THIS BOOK
BELONGS
TO

Ms. Lannell

TEDDY'S NIGHT

LOST

IN THE BUSH

Written & Illustrated by
Bruce Peardon

To my son Ben, in the fervent hope that his and future generations will have the opportunity to enjoy the unique fauna and flora of his homeland, Australia.

Published by the Association of Mouth & Foot Painting Artists
©
ISBN No. 0 907159 42 7

Early one warm summer's evening
  As the sun slipped slowly down,
A family in their horse-drawn cart,
  Rode their way back home from town.

Mother and Father sat up front
As they headed for their farm,
Their sleeping boy lay in the back,
A Teddy tucked under his arm.

But not far away from their home,
The cart wheel hit a big bump,
And Ted was shaken from the back
And fell with an awful thump!

When the family arrived back home,
   The boy was carried to bed,
And the blankets tucked in snugly,
   But nobody missed poor old Ted.

As poor Teddy lay on the road,
   Silvery light came from the moon
And eerie sounds haunted the night —
   Perhaps he'd be rescued soon.

Next morning just as the sun rose,
　　Tom Wombat came waddling along,
And when he saw poor Ted, enquired,
　　"Hey mate, is there something wrong?"

But Teddy could not give an answer,
　　As still on the road he lay,
Because when you're full of stuffing,
　　There isn't much you can say!

Jack Possum peeped from a gum tree
    And watched the scene down below,
Then called out, "Who's the stranger, Tom?"
    Said Wombat, "Blowed if I know."

"I think he's either lost or hurt,"
    Said Tom Wombat with a frown.
"Well I know some First-Aid," said Jack,
    "I'll grab my bag and come down."

Jack examined Teddy, saying,
   "It has got me baffled, Tom;
I don't know if he's sick or well,
   Or just where he could be from!"

"Perhaps," said Wombat to Possum,
   "We'll ask Mope Owl to come here,
He knows most of the animals
   That come from parts far and near."

So Jack sped off and found Mope Owl
Perched in an iron-bark tree,
And told Mope of the strange creature
And asked could he come and see.

After taking a look at Ted
    Said Mope Owl, "I am quite sure,
This fellow doesn't live 'round here,
    I've never seen him before."

Mope Owl for a moment pondered,
    Then said, "Listen to my plan,
Some of our mates may be of help;
    So let's find out if they can."

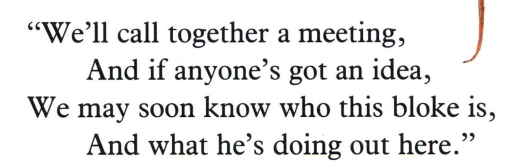

"We'll call together a meeting,
    And if anyone's got an idea,
We may soon know who this bloke is,
    And what he's doing out here."

"So let's go and tell everybody,
    Billy Magpie, Major, Emu . . .
And we'll meet back here very soon
    Then decide what we will do."

"Is it wise to ask old Major?"
        Said Jack, "For as we all know,
He always wants to be in charge,
        And to try and run the show!"

Mope Owl answered quite firmly,
        "Now Jack I'll have you take heed!
The Major is a smart fellow,
        And likely he's who we'll need!"

"So away with you, Jack and Tom,
        There's no time for debate,
Everyone's to be here shortly,
        It's already getting quite late."

"All right," said Wombat and Possum.
And they set about their task,
Whilst Mope flew off through the trees,
To gather all he could ask.

Possum found Tim the Koala,
   Asleep in a blue-gum tree,
And startled Tim when he shouted,
   "No time to explain, follow me!"

Alf Echidna was digging up ants
    When Wombat told him the news.
"Forget your breakfast," said Wombat,
    "There's not a moment to lose!"

Meanwhile, Mope was also busy,
   Inviting all who he knew.
Major, Billy Magpie, Numbat,
   And Katie the Kangaroo.

Soon all the creatures were hurrying
   To where the meeting would be,
And hopefully someone would know
   Poor old Teddy's identity.

When the animals had gathered,
    Jack Possum sat Teddy up,
And Emu said, "If you ask me . . .
    I'd say that's a little pup."

"A pup!" chuckled Kookaburra,
  "Emu, that to me sounds dim;
He looks more like a Koala,
  Perhaps he's your cousin, Tim."

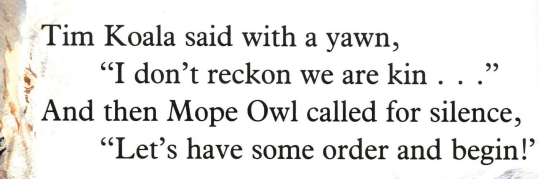

Tim Koala said with a yawn,
        "I don't reckon we are kin . . ."
And then Mope Owl called for silence,
        "Let's have some order and begin!"

"You all will get a chance," said Mope,
        "If there's something you've to say."
"Then I will go first," said Major,
        "And clear this mystery away!"

"That's typical Major," moaned Alf.
    "He always has to go first!
If anyone thinks he knows it all;
    Boring Major is the worst!"

Katie Kangaroo said sternly,
    "Alf Echidna that's unkind!
You'd learn more if you would listen,
    Try and keep that fact in mind!"

"Too right!" warbled Billy Magpie,
　　"Let old Major have his say!"
But without so much as squawk,
　　Major took off and flew away.

"Look what you've done, Alf Echidna!"
　　Said Mope in an angry voice,
"We'll have to coax the Major back;
　　For we don't have any choice . . ."

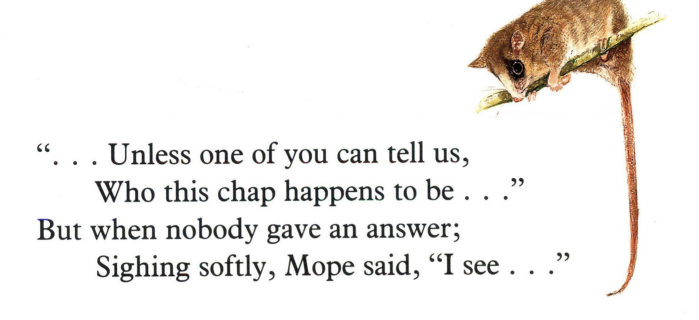

"... Unless one of you can tell us,
    Who this chap happens to be ..."
But when nobody gave an answer;
    Sighing softly, Mope said, "I see ..."

"Major's your best mate," said Mope,
    "So you go and find him, Bill;
And ask him to please come back ...
    I certainly hope he will."

"All right," said Billy, flying off,
　　And he hadn't gone very far,
When he spotted Major sitting
　　On the branch of a coolabah.

"Forget what Alf said," chirped Billy,
　　"He's always in a bad mood.
That lost fellow needs your help,
　　So ignore Alf if he's rude."

Major grinned and said, "You're right,
　　Let's get on with this affair,
For I know where the lost bloke lives,
　　And I'll help to get him there."

"Major, you're a sport," said Billy,
  "I knew we could count on you,
You're just the bird when there's trouble
  To help your friends see it through."

So Major and Billy returned
    To the meeting 'neath the trees,
And from a perch stated Major,
    "Your attention everyone, please!"

"This fellow whom Wombat has found,
    I've seen at a nearby farm,
So we must try to get him home
    Before he can come to harm."

"Are you sure he lives there!" said Mope.
    "As sure as I'm a cockatoo,
'Cause I've seen him with his playmate,
    Whenever I'm passing through."

"Then we must get him home," said Mope,
    "That to me is very clear,
And we'll need someone to hump him,
    So will anyone volunteer?"

"Just a tick!" joked Kookaburra,
    "I've had a brilliant idea,
Alf could let him ride on his back;
    The farm can't be far from here!"

"You can forget it," grumbled Alf,
    "I couldn't carry the weight;
I'm going back to my breakfast,
    So find someone stronger, mate!"

Katie Kangaroo said tartly,
    "Alf you're a cranky old grouch,
I will take the little chap home,
    He can travel in my pouch."

"What a beaut idea!" said Possum,
    "I'll help you tuck him inside."
And all of the creatures agreed,
    It was a safe place to ride.

With Ted comfortably nestled
   In the pouch of Katie 'Roo,
Mope hooted, "Lead the way Major,
   And we will all follow you!"

Soft light filled the little boy's room,
To mark the breaking of day,
And sleepily the boy felt for Ted,
Then let out a cry of dismay!

Father and Mother came running,
    Alert to their child's despair.
"What's the matter love?" said Mother.
    Cried the boy, "Where's Teddy Bear?"

"Now hush your crying," said Father,
    "I'm sure Teddy can be found;
He'll be in the cart or the yard,
    So I'll have a look around."

When Father went to look outside,
    Wasn't surprised when he saw,
Good old Teddy no worse for wear,
    Propped up by the farmhouse door.

Father took Ted in to the boy,
    Saying, "I've found Ted, all right.
We must have dropped him in the dark,
    When I carried you in last night."

But outside the bedroom window,
    Were the ones who really knew,
Why Ted was found on the doorstep,
    And what a trial he'd been through.

43

Then Alf Echidna said, "Major,
    It seems I was terribly wrong,
To be grumpy and call you names,
    For You were right all along."

"That's all right, Alf," said the Major,
    "I shouldn't have taken offence,
For good mates should never argue,
    It just doesn't make any sense."

"There's a lesson we all can learn,"
    Said Mope, "Which I will relate . . .
And that is, through thick and thin,
    We must all co-operate . . .

. . . When it comes to helping someone,
    Nothing should be a bother,
For that's the way we can survive,
    By caring for one another."

And then as the sun rose higher,
     The creatures all slipped away,
For Teddy was now safe at home;
     His bush friends had saved the day.

THE END